For my little pirates, L and W.

First published in 2019 by Page Street Kids,
an imprint of
Page Street Publishing Co.
27 Congress Street, Suite 105
Salem, MA 01970
www.pagestreetpublishing.com

Distributed by Macmillan, sales in Canada by The Canadian Manda Group

19 20 21 22 23 CCO 5 4 3 2 1

ISBN-13: 978-1-62414-655-8
ISBN-10: 1-624-14655-4

CIP data for this book is available from the Library of Congress.

This book was typeset in Sofia Pro.
The illustrations were done in ink and digital color.

Printed and bound in Shenzhen, Guangdong, China

Page Street Publishing uses only materials from suppliers who are committed to responsible and sustainable forest management.

Page Street Publishing protects our planet by donating to nonprofits like The Trustees, which focuses on local land conservation.

MR. SHERMAN'S CLOUD

HABBENINK

Mr. Sherman reluctantly opened his tired eyes. He squirmed down into his bed, twisting and turning until he fell right onto the floor.

"Just great," he grumbled. "Another lousy day."

Suddenly, the room began to get dark, and above his head, Mr. Sherman heard a rumble . . .

He looked up, and there above him, in his bedroom, was a gray, grumbling rain cloud.

The rain started slowly. With each raindrop, Mr. Sherman's mood worsened. Soon it began to pour, drenching him and everything else near him.

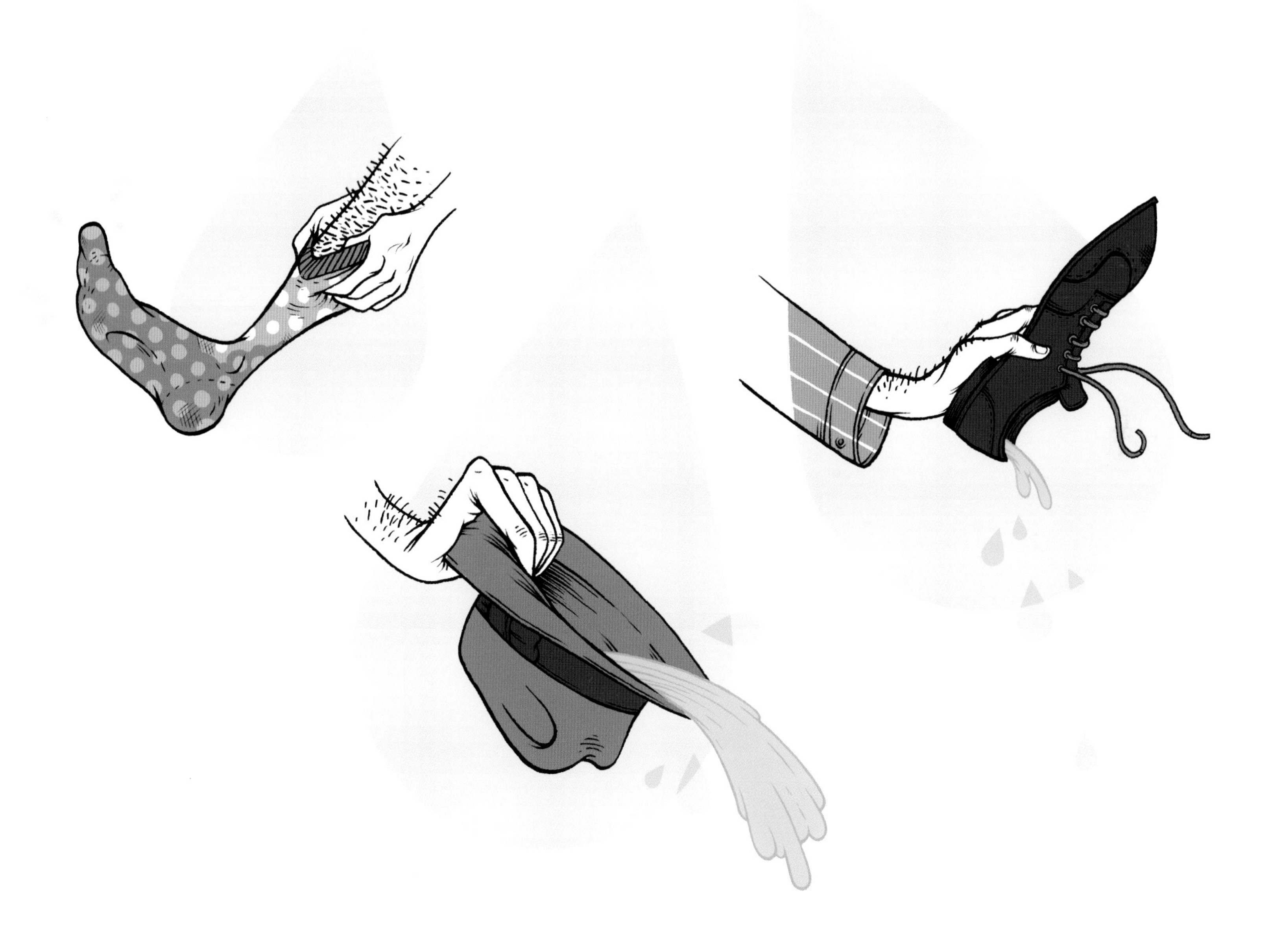

All day long, wherever Mr. Sherman went,
the cloud came too.

No matter what he did,
he couldn't seem
to get rid of it.

The rain began to soak the people around Mr. Sherman too, but they didn't seem to be nearly as bothered by it as he was. One person even offered him an umbrella.

"It's no use!" he complained,
pushing the umbrella away.
"This day is ruined!"

Off he sloshed with
the cloud following above him.

All alone, Mr. Sherman looked gloomily at the river of rainwater leading back down the street. It flowed past the markets and bus stops, through the park, and all the way back into his house.

Some people stepped into the water, and clouds started to form above their heads too. But to Mr. Sherman's surprise, their clouds didn't darken or rain. Just a brief bit of shade, and then they were gone.

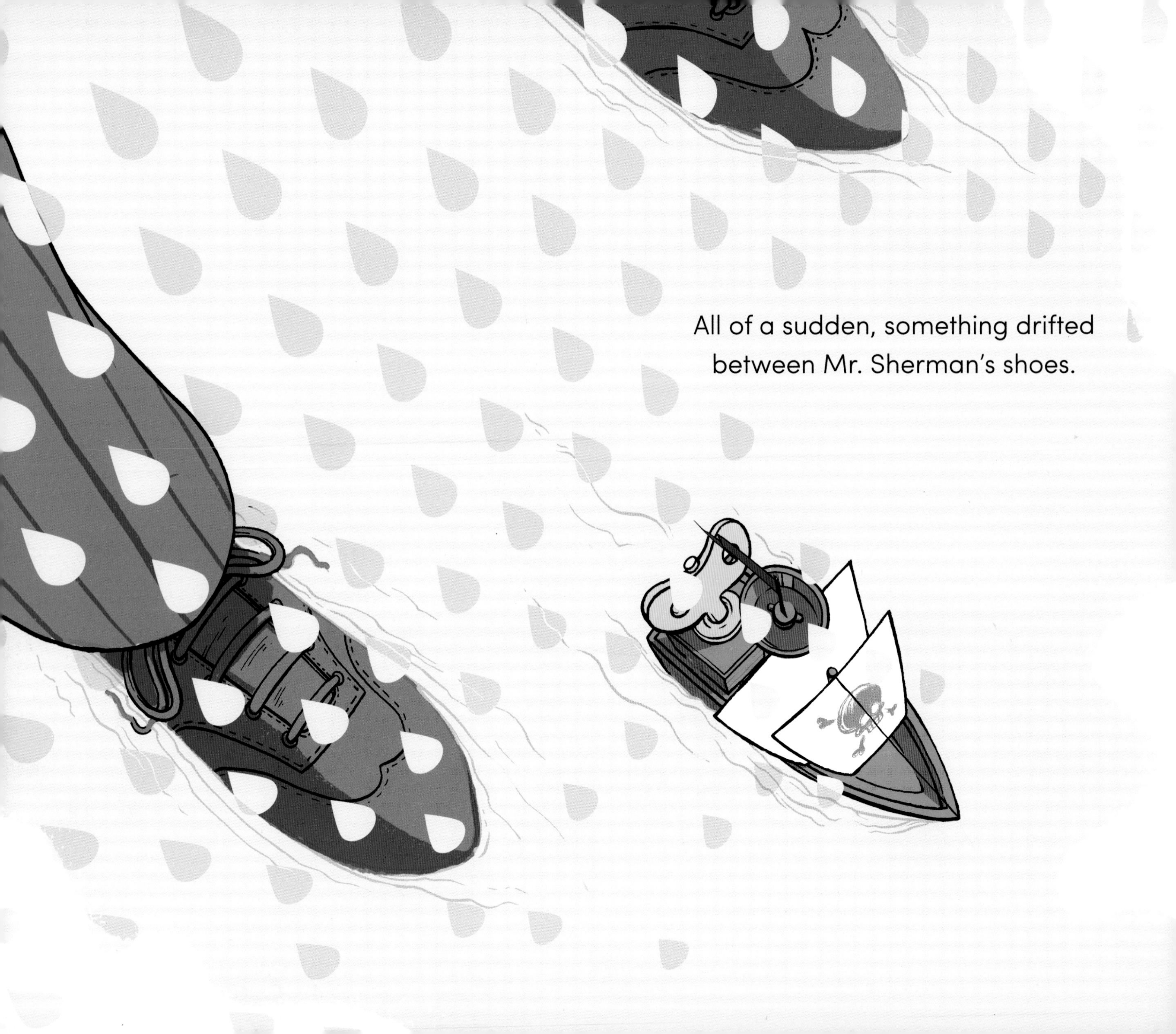

All of a sudden, something drifted
between Mr. Sherman's shoes.

"Ahoy, matey! Look out!"
chirped a voice.

"That's it!" Mr. Sherman fumed, as he punched and kicked at the growing puddle of water.

"Sorry about your hat . . . ,"
said the little girl holding it out.

"Too bad it's not a pirate's hat!" the boy in the cape chimed in. "We're pirates today, and we sure could use another member in our crew."

"Yeah, it's the best day ever to be a pirate!" added the last pirate.

"Best day ever?" scoffed Mr. Sherman. "This rain cloud has been soaking me all day!"

"Whoa! Uh, I mean . . . 'Shiver me timbers!'"
one pirate exclaimed.
"You mean, this is your rain cloud?"

"Well, yes . . . I guess so,"
replied Mr. Sherman.

They gasped, staring up at the cloud . . .
"Hooray! Thanks for the rain!"
they cheered.

They helped Mr. Sherman to his feet
and smothered him in a hug.

Then, as quickly as they had appeared,
they ran off, splashing after their
toys that had floated away.

Mr. Sherman stood there, stunned and sopping.
"Thanks . . . for the rain?"

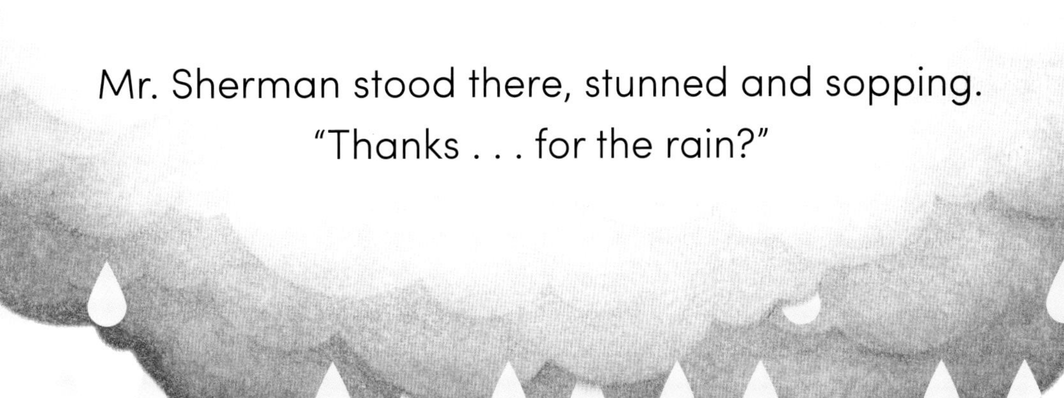

Mr. Sherman watched the rain drip
off his hat onto the ground and
noticed something small, something . . .
beautiful?

At his feet, yellow flowers soaked up the rain and reached toward the sun. All around him, the world was looking fresh and new.

"Maybe things aren't so bad after all,"
he thought to himself.

The rain began to stop
and the cloud started to shrink.

Looking up at where the cloud had been,
Mr. Sherman squinted at the bright sky.

"Maybe I just needed a little bit of a storm
to help me see the sunshine," he considered,
as he sloshed happily down the street.

Rain or shine, today was going to be
a great day.